cloverleaf books™

Stories with Character

We All Have Value
A Story of Respect

Mari Schuh

illustrated by **Mike Byrne**

M MILLBROOK PRESS • MINNEAPOLIS

To the amazing students and teachers
of St. John Vianney School —M.S.

To Joe & Benji —M.B.

Millbrook Press
A division of Lerner Publishing Group, Inc.
241 First Avenue North
Minneapolis, MN 55401 USA

For reading levels and more information, look up this title at www.
lernerbooks.com.

Main body text set in Slappy Inline 22/28.
Typeface provided by T26.

Library of Congress Cataloging-in-Publication Data

Names: Schuh, Mari C., 1975– author. | Byrne, Mike, 1979– illustrator.
Title: We all have value : a story of respect / Mari Schuh, Mike Byrne.
Description: Minneapolis : Millbrook Press, [2018] | Series: Cloverleaf
    Books—stories with character | Includes bibliographical references and
    index.
Identifiers: LCCN 2017012474 (print) | LCCN 2017026902 (ebook) |
    ISBN 9781512498264 (eb pdf) | ISBN 9781512486506 (lb : alk. paper)
Subjects: LCSH: Respect—Juvenile literature. | Respect for persons—Juvenile
    literature.
Classification: LCC BJ1533.R4 (ebook) | LCC BJ1533.R4 .S384 2018 (print) |
    DDC 179/.9—dc23

LC record available at https://lccn.loc.gov/2017012474

Manufactured in the United States of America
2-46346-33214-7/2/2018

TABLE OF CONTENTS

Chapter One

Waiting Our Turn

My friend Pete and I are so excited!
It's pizza day in the lunchroom today.

Pizza is our favorite food!

5

"Idil! I want to get the biggest slice!" Pete tells me.
He moves right to the front of the line.

"Pete, it was Ben's turn," I say.
"Yeah, but I love pizza!" Pete replies.

Being respectful means
waiting your turn.

After lunch, we break into groups to work on our science projects.

"Hey, Ben, what do you think this wooden block is going to do in water? Float or sink?" asks Sofia, our group's leader.

"Hmmm . . . I think it will . . ." Ben stops to think.

"Float! It will float!" Pete interrupts.

Letting others finish speaking before you speak shows respect.

Sofia puts the block in water to test it out. "Yep. The block floats," she says, writing down our group's results. "But I was asking Ben."

Chapter Two

Thinking of Others

Before we know it, it's time for recess.
Ty, Chloe, and I get ready to play Four Square.
"Can I play too?" asks Ben.

"No, I want to play! And only four can play this game," says Pete.

Letting everyone join in is respectful.

After winning the first game, Chloe decides she's done playing Four Square. "I'm going to shoot hoops with Ben," she tells us.

"Me too!" I say.

"But, you guys, I still want to play Four Square," Pete says.

"Sorry, Pete, I want to have a chance to play with Ben," I answer.

Chapter Three

Showing Respect

On the bus ride home, Pete asks me why
I didn't keep playing Four Square.

"It's not that I didn't want to play with you," I say. "But Ben didn't have much fun today. He wanted to play, and I wanted to play with him too. How would you feel if someone left you out of things?"

STOP

Pete frowns. "Not very good, I guess," he says.

"Exactly," I reply.
"Everyone has value, you know."

19

As we get off the bus, Pete walks up to Ben. "Ben, I'm **really sorry** I wasn't very nice to you today. How about we play Four Square together tomorrow?"

"That'd be fun!" Ben says.
"Maybe the three of us can have lunch together too," I add.

"Awesome!" Ben and Pete say at the same time. I laugh. I can tell Ben and Pete are going to be great friends.

STOP

Four Square Respect Activity

It's important to show respect for others. Here's a way to think about how you can show respect throughout your day:

What You Will Need
a pencil
a large, blank sheet of paper

What You Will Do

1) Draw a big square that fills up almost all of the page.

2) Divide that square into four smaller squares by drawing one line from left to right and one line from top to bottom.

3) Near the top of each square, write one of these headings:

- At School

- Around Town

- With Family

- With Friends

4) Then, in each square, write three ways you can show respect at that place or with those people. Ask an adult or friend for some ideas if you need help.

GLOSSARY

Four Square: a game played with one ball and four players on a court that's divided into four squares

interrupt: to start talking before someone else is done talking

recess: a short break during the school day when kids can play

respectful: showing kindness and consideration for another person

science: the study of nature and the physical world

BOOKS

Boritzer, Etan. *What Is Respect?* Santa Monica, CA: Veronica Lane Books, 2016. Discover ways to respect yourself, others, animals, and objects through everyday examples.

Donovan, Sandy. *How Can I Deal with Bullying? A Book about Respect.* Minneapolis: Lerner Publications, 2014. Read this book to learn how to handle difficult situations by showing respect.

Johnson, Kristin. *In It Together: A Story of Fairness*. Minneapolis: Millbrook Press, 2018. Read about another important character value—fairness, or the ability to treat everyone the same way and not play favorites.

WEBSITES

Respect
http://characterfirsteducation.com/c/curriculum-detail/2153253
Visit this website and watch the videos to learn more about respect.

Respect Worksheet
http://www.worksheetplace.com/mf_pdf/charad.pdf
Answer the questions on this worksheet to share what you know about respect.

What Is Respect?
http://talkingtreebooks.com/docs/worksheet/character-ed-worksheet-what-is-respect.pdf
Read this worksheet and decide if people in different situations are showing respect.